OSCAR

Don't miss any of these other stories by Ellen Miles!

THE PUPPY PLACE

OSCAR

ELLEN MILES

SCHOLASTIC INC.

For everyone who has had to say good-bye to a beloved pet.

ISBN 978-0-545-46241-9

Cover art by Tim O'Brien
Original cover design by Steve Scott

12 11 10 9 8 7 6 5 4 3 2 1   13 14 15 16 17 18/0

Printed in the U.S.A.   40

First printing, January 2013

CHAPTER ONE

"Does anybody want one more pancake?" Dad stood by the stove with a spatula in his hand.

"No, thanks," said Lizzie.

"No, thanks," said her younger brother Charles, at exactly the same time.

They stared at each other. "Pickle Jinx!" yelled Charles.

Lizzie thought fast. She was ready this time. "Beautiful Genius," she said. Then she started to laugh.

The Bean started to giggle, too. He banged his fork on his syrup-smeared plate. "Bootifulgeeny!" he yelled. The Bean was Lizzie's youngest brother.

His real name was Adam, but nobody ever called him that. He would probably be the Bean forever, or at least until he started kindergarten.

Charles groaned. "C'mon, Lizzie —" he began.

Lizzie glared at him.

Charles rolled his eyes. "I mean, come on. Beautiful Genius. Really? Are you sure about that?"

Lizzie ran a finger through a puddle of syrup on her plate. She licked her finger, smiled, and nodded. "Yup," she said. "That's how Pickle Jinx works, remember? Whatever word I say first after you say 'Pickle Jinx,' that's what you have to call me for the rest of the day." Pickle Jinx was all the rage in Lizzie's fourth-grade class, and in Charles's second-grade class, too.

"Yeah, I remember." Charles slumped in his seat. "I liked it better the time you said, 'No, Wait!'"

Lizzie grinned at him. That was exactly why she'd vowed to be prepared for the next Pickle Jinx.

Mom pushed her chair back. "Well, whatever you two want to call each other, just do it quietly, please. I'm looking forward to a nice, relaxing Sunday. All I want to do is lie on the couch with a bellyful of pancakes and work on the crossword."

"I'll clear the table," Lizzie volunteered.

"Really?" Mom looked surprised. "Thanks! That would be great. That's very nice of you, Lizzie." She picked up the thick newspaper and, yawning, headed for the living room. Dad ruffled Lizzie's hair and followed Mom out of the kitchen.

As soon as her parents were out of sight, Lizzie smiled down at Buddy, the adorable brown-and-white puppy sitting near her chair. His brown eyes shone with hope as he stared back at her, his brow wrinkled in the cutest "how-can-you-resist-me?" look.

Buddy was the best puppy ever — and Lizzie had known a lot of puppies to compare him to. The Petersons fostered puppies. They took care of pups who needed homes, and found each one the perfect forever family. They'd cared for wild puppies and mellow pups, big ones and tiny ones. But most of them stayed for just a few days or a few weeks. Buddy was the only one who had stayed forever. He was part of the Peterson family.

Lizzie was dog-crazy. She loved all dogs, and all puppies. But there was no question that she loved Buddy best. "Guess what?" Lizzie whispered to him now. She reached for her plate.

"Lizzie!" said Charles. "You're not going to —"

Lizzie swiveled her head around to give Charles a look.

Charles cleared his throat. "I mean, Beautiful Genius," he mumbled. "You know Mom says we're not allowed to let Buddy lick our plates."

Lizzie put a finger over her lips. "Shhh," she said. "Just this once. Maple syrup is his favorite treat ever." Lizzie knew it was a safe treat, too. Some things weren't good for dogs, like chocolate or grapes, but a few drizzles of maple syrup would be fine.

Charles hesitated. He looked down at Buddy, who stared back and put a paw on Charles's leg. Then Charles nodded. Lizzie knew that he couldn't resist Buddy, either. "Okay," he said, grinning at her as they both put their plates down on the floor. Buddy went to work, licking so hard that he pushed Lizzie's plate clear across the kitchen.

"Ha!" yelled the Bean. "Buddy likes syrup!"

"Shhh, shhh." Lizzie put a finger to her lips. "Buddy won't get syrup if Mommy hears you."

The Bean put both hands over his mouth and watched, his eyes dancing, as Buddy licked every drop of syrup off Lizzie's plate, then went after Charles's. "Mine, too!" he said, holding up his plate so that syrup began to drip onto his lap.

Quickly, Lizzie grabbed it and put it down for Buddy. "There you go," she said lovingly. Buddy's tail wagged so hard that it thumped against Lizzie's chair. He vacuumed up every bit of syrup, then sat back and licked his chops as he looked hopefully at Lizzie. "That's it," she said, holding up her hands. Mom and Dad never seemed to end up with extra syrup on their plates.

She hummed as she cleared the table and stuck the dishes into the dishwasher. Like her mom, she was looking forward to a nice, relaxing Sunday. Lizzie had been really busy lately, between school, volunteering at the animal shelter, and her dog-walking business. She and her best friend, Maria, were partners in AAA Dynamic Dog Walkers, and they walked about a dozen dogs every single day after school. Even dog-crazy Lizzie had to admit that sometimes it all seemed like a little too much.

"Hey, Lizzie, want to —" This time, Charles stopped himself. "I mean, hey, Beautiful Genius, want to play catch out back?"

"No, thanks." Lizzie was really enjoying her Pickle Jinx name. "I'm going to work on my scrapbook." Lizzie kept a scrapbook of all the puppies the Petersons had fostered, and it needed updating.

She was up in her room, pasting in a picture of a sweet, energetic chocolate Lab named Cocoa, when the phone rang. "Lizzie!" called her mom after a few minutes. "It's your aunt Amanda. She needs your help with a puppy."

CHAPTER TWO

"A puppy?" Lizzie asked her aunt when she'd picked up the phone in her mom's study. "What kind? Are we going to foster it? How old?"

"I'll explain everything when you get here," said Aunt Amanda. "Can I send your uncle over to pick you up and bring you to Bowser's?"

Lizzie thought for a moment. She had really been looking forward to some quiet time at home. Plus, there was the total awesomeness of having Charles call her Beautiful Genius all day. But Aunt Amanda was hard to resist. She ran a doggy daycare center called Bowser's Backyard (named after her big old golden retriever), and she knew more about dogs than anybody in the world. Lizzie had learned a lot from her.

Lizzie loved to help out at Bowser's Backyard, but lately she'd been too busy with her dog-walking business to be able spend much time there on weekday afternoons, when Bowser's was full of dogs. It was unusual for Aunt Amanda to need her help on a weekend, when things were quieter. Lizzie was curious. What was up with this puppy?

"Lizzie?" Aunt Amanda asked. "What do you say?"

"Sure," said Lizzie. "I'll be ready when Uncle James gets here." She hung up and went back to her room to put away her scrapbook stuff. Then she headed downstairs to let her parents know where she was going.

A few minutes later, Lizzie heard a honk outside. She checked out the living-room window and saw the Bowser Mobile, with its POOCHES license plate, pulled up in front. "That's Uncle James," she told her parents. "I'll see you later."

"Don't come home with a puppy," her mom said drowsily. She lay on the couch with newspapers strewn all around her.

"Bye!" said Lizzie. She wasn't promising anything.

"Later, Lizzie," said Charles, who was sprawled in the middle of the living-room floor, reading the Sunday comics to Buddy and the Bean.

Lizzie put her hands on her hips and glared at her brother.

"See ya, Beautiful Genius," Charles said, rolling his eyes.

"Bootifulgeenie," echoed the Bean. "Mootiful-beenie. Gootifuldeenie," he chanted, laughing his googly laugh.

"That's better." Lizzie, the Beautiful Genius, held her head high as she stepped out to meet Uncle James.

"Hey there," he said as she climbed into the van. "Glad you could help out. I've got a billion chores to do today, and we have no staff on weekends, so your aunt's stuck by herself."

"Where's the puppy?" asked Lizzie. "And what's the big problem? It's not like you usually have a ton of dogs on the weekends."

"We're picking him up right now," her uncle said. "And the problem isn't how many dogs we have. It's how well they get along." He turned onto a wide, quiet street lined with big houses set back from the road. "Help me look for number thirty-eight," he said. "That's Oscar's place."

"Oscar!" Lizzie said. "What a great name for a puppy. What breed is he?"

"That breed stuff is more your aunt's specialty," said Uncle James, shrugging. "He's a little guy, with kind of wiry black-and-gray hair. He has this funny mustache and beard, and bushy eyebrows."

"Sounds like a schnauzer!" said Lizzie. "Cool!" Dog breeds were her specialty, too. Every night she studied her "Dog Breeds of the World" poster, and she had no trouble telling a Nova Scotia duck tolling retriever from a Chesapeake Bay retriever.

"And there he is right now," said Uncle James as he pulled over in front of a big brick house with white pillars. A woman stood in the front yard, holding one end of a red leash. On the other end of the leash was the most adorable puppy.

"Oh, look at him!" cried Lizzie. As soon as the van came to a stop, she unbuckled and climbed out. She couldn't wait to get a closer look. The puppy was like a little cartoon character, with his mustache, long wiry beard, and wild eyebrows. As Lizzie approached, he bounced up and down at the end of his leash on stiff, springy legs, letting out happy little woofs.

"This is Oscar," said the woman. "And I'm Susannah."

"Susannah, this is Lizzie," said Uncle James. "She's our niece, and she's terrific with dogs. She's going to help out with Oscar today."

"Hi, Susannah. Hi, Oscar," Lizzie said as she knelt to pet the puppy.

Oscar climbed right up onto her and licked her face, tickling her cheek with his bristly mustache.

Hello! Who might you be? You smell absolutely delectable!

Susannah looked surprised. "Wow, he really likes you! Schnauzers are usually a little shy with strangers." She handed his leash to Lizzie. "Please tell Amanda how much we appreciate this. We're really at our wits' end. We love Oscar, but it's just not fair to Sarge."

"Sarge?" Lizzie asked.

Susannah pointed toward the house. Lizzie saw a dog watching them from a picture window. He looked like a German shepherd. "Oscar and Sarge just can't seem to get along," she said. "We've had Sarge for three years, and he's the sweetest guy ever. He's our darling. We adopted Oscar because we thought Sarge would like a friend. But it seems as if we brought home an enemy instead."

Lizzie looked down at the puppy in her arms. Who wouldn't get along with this little goofball? Maybe Sarge was just jealous, the way Buddy once was when the Petersons had been fostering a miniature poodle named Sweetie. Buddy couldn't stand it when anybody paid attention to that puppy. Lizzie nuzzled her cheek against Oscar's.

"We love Oscar," said Susannah. He's smart, he's funny, and he's terrific with my two little boys, Thomas and Peter. I thought things were improving between him and Sarge, but then this morning they just kept getting into squabbles." She held up her hands. "Maybe it's hopeless."

Lizzie stood up, holding Oscar. "Well, Sarge can have a nice quiet day, anyway. We'll take good care of Oscar."

Susannah reached out to pet the funny little pup. "Bye, baby," she murmured. "You have fun at Bowser's." She held his paw for a long moment, her face very serious. Then she turned away. Lizzie had the funny feeling that Susannah might be fighting back tears.

Lizzie brought Oscar back to the van and climbed inside. "I still don't get why Aunt Amanda needed my help," she said to Uncle James. "How much trouble could this puppy be?"

"You'll see," said Uncle James as he started up the van.

CHAPTER THREE

When they arrived at Bowser's Backyard, Uncle James told Lizzie to stay in the car with Oscar for a moment while he went in to make sure Aunt Amanda was ready for them. Lizzie was happy to sit with Oscar. He was such a cutie, and she could already see that Susannah was right: he was smart, too. His eyes were watchful and bright. He reminded her of a wise old man, with those bushy eyebrows and that long beard. His perky ears gave him an alert look, and his stocky body was athletic and ready for action. She stroked his wiry hair, feeling the softer undercoat beneath it when she scratched his chest.

"You're a funny little guy," she whispered to him. He leaned against her, and she could tell that he felt relaxed and comfortable on her lap.

When Aunt Amanda came out to get them, Oscar wagged his stubby tail and licked her face. "Hello, sweetie," she said as she petted him. "What are we going to do with you? Why can't you be as friendly with dogs as you are with people?" She turned to Lizzie. "Isn't he great?" she asked. "He's smart, he's cute, he's terrific with kids. He just needs to learn to get along with other dogs."

"You mean it's not just Sarge he squabbles with?" Lizzie asked.

Aunt Amanda shook her head as she led Lizzie and Oscar into the building and down an empty hallway. "He doesn't seem to like most other dogs. And when he growls or shows his teeth, he scares some of my other customers."

"That's not good," said Lizzie.

"Not good at all," agreed Aunt Amanda. "Oscar isn't exactly what we would call an aggressive dog — not yet. He's not mean, or a biter. If he were, I wouldn't allow him here. He'd never hurt another dog — at least, I don't think he would. He just acts like a grouch sometimes. But if he does not learn to get along with other dogs, it could turn into a real problem. People who have aggressive dogs can't go to dog parks, or trust their dogs anywhere in public."

Aunt Amanda opened the door to the indoor play area, where there were slides and tunnels and toys of every kind strewn over the rubber mat–covered floor. "I only have five dogs to take care of today," she said. "Right now they're all outside, so we can let Oscar run around in here for a while. I thought you could be in charge of him so I can give the other dogs some attention."

Lizzie unclipped Oscar's leash, and he began to roam around the room, checking out all the toys. "Why do you think he acts grouchy?" Lizzie asked. She still couldn't imagine Oscar growling at anybody. He seemed like such a sweetheart. She watched him nudge an oversized blue-and-white soccer ball along the floor, scampering behind it as it rolled.

Aunt Amanda shrugged. "Some dogs are aggressive because they're afraid. I don't think that's the case with Oscar. He may not have been socialized as a puppy, maybe because he left his mom too early or didn't get to play enough with his brothers and sisters. Sometimes I think he's just confused. He really just wants to play, but he has that terrier personality."

Lizzie knew what that meant. "You mean, even though he's small he thinks he's a big tough dog?"

"Exactly," said Aunt Amanda. "He's fearless, and he loves to chase moving things. He gets too rough with Sarge, and Sarge gets upset. According to Susannah, when he was a tiny puppy it wasn't so bad. But he's six months old now, and he's started to challenge Sarge a little."

"Challenge him?" Lizzie asked. "How do you mean?" Oscar nosed the soccer ball in her direction and she kicked it away so he could chase it.

"He's just always competing with Sarge," said Aunt Amanda. "For attention from the family, for toys, for space inside the house. Susannah said he's always trying to be the first one out the door, shoving Sarge out of the way."

"Maybe he needs to be the only dog in a family," Lizzie said. She smiled as she watched Oscar push the ball back toward her.

"That's what I've been thinking," said Aunt

Amanda. "And I believe that I've almost convinced Susannah of that, too. She told me that she was planning to sit down with the family and have a long talk about Oscar's future."

Lizzie remembered the way Susannah had said good-bye to Oscar, so sadly. She was sorry for Susannah, but she felt her own heart lift a little. Maybe there was a new foster puppy in her future! "You mean, they might decide to give him up?"

Aunt Amanda nodded. "The family loves Oscar. But the constant bickering between him and Sarge is making everyone nuts, and Sarge is their top priority, since they've had him longer."

"Can't they try training Oscar?" Lizzie watched the little pup bounce around on his stiff, springy legs. Now he was playing with a rope toy. He picked it up and shook it, tossed it into the air, let it fall, looked at it for a moment, then pounced and started the whole routine over again. Lizzie couldn't help giggling at his antics. He must have heard her laugh, because he looked over at her and waggled his eyebrows.

Is there something amusing going on?

Lizzie stifled her laughter. Oscar looked so dignified, with his long beard.

"Susannah has done a lot of obedience training with him. She feels like she and her husband have done everything they can," said Aunt Amanda. "But she's really busy. She thought we could help him here, that he could meet other dogs and get to know them. I've tried, but it's not easy when I'm handling thirty dogs or more on weekdays."

Just then, the door behind them opened and Uncle James walked in — with Bowser trotting by his side.

"We're going to head home," he said to Aunt Amanda. "Just wanted to —"

But he didn't have the chance to finish his sentence. When Oscar spotted the other dog, he let out a few woofs, in a deeper voice than Lizzie would have expected. Then the wiry pup charged at top speed toward the golden retriever at Uncle James's side, ears back and teeth showing.

CHAPTER FOUR

"No, Oscar! Down!" Aunt Amanda yelled.

Uncle James yanked Bowser back through the door and shut it quickly.

Oscar looked bewildered, but he obeyed Aunt Amanda's command and plopped to the floor, still grumbling under his breath. He looked up at her from beneath his bushy eyebrows.

I didn't intend to do anything wrong. I was just hoping for a bit of fun.

"Wow," said Lizzie. Her heart was still beating fast. "That was kind of scary."

Aunt Amanda nodded. "And he's just a puppy. Imagine if he still behaves that way when he's full-grown. Someone is going to have to spend a lot of time and effort working with him, to break him of his bad habits."

"He lay down when you asked him to." Lizzie pointed at Oscar, who still lay on the rubber mat–covered floor, his ears perked as he waited for the next command.

"His obedience training pays off," said Aunt Amanda. "And asking him to do something, whether it's lie down or sit or stay, is a great way to distract him and give him something else to think about." She signaled to Oscar that it was okay to get up, and he bounced to his feet.

"Just like when I was trying to teach Teddy not to bark all the time," Lizzie said, remembering the noisy Pomeranian pup her family had fostered. "If I asked him to sit, or do a trick, he would stop barking. At least for a few seconds."

Aunt Amanda looked at Lizzie. "You did a great job with that puppy," she said. "Are you ready for another challenge?"

"You mean . . . ?" Lizzie asked.

Aunt Amanda nodded. "I'm going to call Susannah. I'm guessing that her family has come to the same conclusion I have — that Oscar probably needs to find a new home. It may take a while to find him one — and that's where your family comes in. Do you think you could foster Oscar?"

Lizzie looked at the wiry-haired pup. What a cutie! He was playing with a big orange-and-black stuffed tiger he'd found in a corner. He clutched it between his paws and gnawed gently on its head, making the squeaker inside squeal.

But Lizzie couldn't forget the way he'd charged at Bowser.

Oscar might be a bigger challenge than she — or her family — was ready for. And what about Buddy? If it wasn't fair to Sarge to have Oscar around, it wouldn't be fair to Buddy, either. Then again, Buddy had always gotten along with their other foster puppies — except for that time when he was jealous of Sweetie. Maybe he and Oscar could be friends. Anyway, it was only temporary. It wasn't as if Oscar would be coming to live with them forever.

Lizzie took a deep breath. "If that's what Susannah and her family want, and if I can talk *my* family into it, then the answer is yes. I'd like to foster Oscar," she told her aunt.

When Dad came to pick Lizzie up later that afternoon, she was waiting for him out front —

holding Oscar's leash. "That's my dad," she told Oscar. She bent down to whisper into the puppy's ear. "Be extra nice, okay?"

Oscar wagged his tail and licked her face. He gazed steadily into her eyes with a wise look.

I promise to behave in an appropriate manner, as long as you keep petting me!

"Hold on, hold on," said Dad when he saw the pup. "You heard what your mother said. No coming home with puppies." But he got out of his truck and knelt to say hello to Oscar. Lizzie smiled to herself. Her dad loved puppies almost as much as she did.

"Oscar is a special case," Lizzie told him. "I know we need to talk it over, but no matter what, he really needs a place to stay tonight." She explained that when Aunt Amanda had called

Susannah, they'd both agreed that Oscar needed a new home. Susannah had been crying on the phone. She said that once her family had made the decision, she thought it would be easier if Oscar did not come back that night. "And we don't want him to spend the night in a kennel, here or at Caring Paws, do we?" Lizzie asked her dad.

Dad hesitated. "Well, he's awful cute," he finally said. "Friendly, too," he added with a laugh as Oscar leaned against him and licked his hand.

"He loves people," Lizzie agreed. She wasn't exactly lying, was she? She decided to wait until they were on the way home to explain more to Dad about exactly why Oscar needed to find a new family. She got Oscar settled in the backseat of Dad's red pickup, then climbed in and buckled her seat belt.

Once they were driving, Lizzie told Dad about Oscar's problem with other dogs. Dad put the brakes on and pulled over to the side of the road. "Lizzie," he began.

"I know, I know," she said, holding up her hands. "But remember. He's not really a mean dog. He just acts that way sometimes. All he needs is some love and training. Please, let's just bring him home. We'll work it out, I know we will. And he needs our help."

Dad glanced into the rearview mirror. Lizzie turned around to look at Oscar, too. The little schnauzer cocked his head and put up a pleading paw. Lizzie grinned. She knew Dad couldn't resist that.

When they pulled into the driveway, Dad gave Lizzie a serious look. "Wait here with Oscar for a few minutes. I want to get Buddy into the den with the door closed. I think it'll be safest just to keep the puppies separated for the short time that Oscar is with us."

Lizzie nodded. She and Oscar sat quietly, waiting until Dad gave her the okay sign from the window. "Be on your best behavior," she warned him when she opened the back door to let him inside.

When she walked into the living room, the Bean gave a shriek from where he sat in Dad's lap. "A puppy!" he yelled.

"A puppy!" said Charles at the same time.

Mom sat up straight on the couch. "A puppy?" she chimed in.

"Pickle Jinx!" cried Lizzie.

And for the rest of that day, they all had new names: The Bean was "Puppypuppypuppy." Charles was "Oh, cool!" And her mother was "Elizabeth-Maude-Peterson-how-could-you!"

CHAPTER FIVE

A Triple Pickle Jinx didn't turn out to be as fun as Lizzie had imagined it would be. First of all, Charles wouldn't even answer to his name. He said the whole thing didn't count because Lizzie wasn't really one of the Pickle Jinxers. The Bean liked his name, but he was off to a bath and bed right after dinner, so Lizzie didn't get to use it much.

And calling Mom "Elizabeth-Maude-Peterson-how-could-you!" got old pretty fast. Like, after one time. Especially when Lizzie also had to spend so much time explaining how their family was Oscar's only hope, and how she would make sure that Buddy got enough attention, even if he did have to be shut up in a room half the time while Oscar was there (the other half they would keep Oscar shut up, which seemed fair), and a bunch of other stuff to get her family to agree to keep Oscar until they could find him a forever home.

"Which better not take too long," were Mom's last words on the topic.

The next afternoon, Lizzie had to spend even more time explaining to Charles why he should help her by watching Oscar and playing with him in the backyard. "That way I can take Buddy along while Maria and I walk dogs," she said.

"I don't get why you can't take Oscar, so I can play with Buddy," Charles said.

"Because." Lizzie sighed. Wasn't it obvious? "Because Oscar doesn't get along with other dogs."

"It was your idea to foster him," Charles reminded her. "But I'll make you a deal. I'll stay with Oscar if you promise that next time we have a Pickle Jinx I get to call you whatever I want. Or you have to call me . . . let's see. How about Most Perfect Brother? Even without a Pickle Jinx. Like — starting now."

Lizzie nodded wearily. "Fine. Whatever, Most Perfect Brother." As soon as Charles took Oscar into the backyard, she grabbed Buddy's leash and hurried out to meet Maria.

Maria did not make things easy, either. "Oh," she said. "You brought Buddy." She didn't say much else until they had picked up their first client, a German shepherd named Tank. "It always complicates things when you bring another dog along," Maria said finally, as Tank trotted along next to her. He was a strong young dog who walked very nicely as long as he was wearing his head harness.

Lizzie stared at her friend. "I thought you, of all people, would understand," she said. During recess that day, she'd told Maria all about "the Oscar situation." "Buddy deserves some extra attention, since we have to keep him and Oscar apart."

Maria shrugged. "Yeah. I understand," she said. "I understand that whatever you're doing is the most important thing, and if it makes more work for me, that's okay. In your mind, anyway."

Ouch. Lizzie felt the sting of Maria's words. She opened her mouth, then shut it again. She really didn't want to get into a fight with her best friend, especially when they had a business to run together. Anyway, she couldn't deny that it was true. Maria had taken up the slack — or had been forced to find extra help — for AAA Dynamic

Dog Walkers a few times recently, when Lizzie was busy with foster puppies who needed lots of attention.

"There are other things I'd like to be doing, too, you know." Maria sounded a little less mad now. "I miss being at the stables all the time, for one thing. Sometimes I wonder about this business. I wonder if we've bitten off more than we can chew."

Lizzie pictured herself and Maria as puppies, each biting into one end of a giant T-bone steak. She couldn't help herself. She burst into giggles. "I'm sorry," she said. "I know you're being serious."

She told Maria what she'd imagined, and Maria laughed, too. "You're right, it sounds funny. It's just something my mom says," she said.

Lizzie had to admit that Maria was right. It did complicate things when Lizzie had another dog along. Even Buddy, who was well behaved. It made it hard for Lizzie to walk two other dogs, for example. Plus, Buddy wanted to sniff and play with all the other dogs, which made each walk take longer than it should. "Let's just split up and finish the rest separately," she said to Maria after they'd walked the first six dogs. "I'll do Dottie and Scruffy and Ginger, deal?"

"Deal," said Maria. They linked pinkies and shook.

"And we'll figure out a way to make our business work better," Lizzie promised. "Soon. As soon as I find a home for Oscar." She knew she had to do whatever it took to keep her business partner — and her best friend — happy.

Lizzie headed for Dottie's house. Dottie was a Dalmatian who was almost totally deaf. She was a sweet girl, and Lizzie had enjoyed learning hand signals as a way of communicating with her. Come to think of it, though, Dottie did not get along with all dogs. She generally liked smaller ones, so Lizzie knew it was okay to bring Buddy along when she walked Dottie. But when she was around big dogs, like Tank and Atlas, Dottie would get all growly, showing her teeth. Dottie acted grouchy sometimes, just like Oscar.

Lizzie watched carefully as Buddy and Dottie sniffed each other. First they both stood very, very still as they touched noses. Then their tails began to wag, almost as if they were saying, "Okay, everything's fine between us." Buddy put his backside in the air and splayed his front legs in front of him, in the "want-to-play?" position, and Dottie mimicked his move. They had a brief, non-growly wrestling match, then jumped to their feet and looked expectantly at Lizzie. She laughed. "I guess you're ready for your walk," she said. "Let's go."

After she'd brought Dottie home, Lizzie fetched Scruffy, the little Morkie (that meant Maltese plus Yorkie) pup. He looked a little like a dirty white mop — a very *cute* dirty white mop. He and Buddy also made friends right away, and soon they were prancing down the street carrying a big stick together, tails waving proudly.

Lizzie watched, and she thought. Poor Oscar might never get to have doggy friends like this unless he learned how to get along with other dogs. But how was that going to happen if Aunt Amanda kept him separate from all her other clients, and the Petersons kept him separate from Buddy?

Then she had an idea. What about Ginger?

CHAPTER SIX

It wasn't just an idea. It was a *great* idea. After all, Oscar needed a friend, and Ginger would be perfect! Aunt Amanda had told Lizzie that Oscar was grouchier with boy dogs than with girl dogs. And part of his problem was that he wanted to be top dog. Well, Ginger was a girl dog. And Lizzie was sure that Ginger wouldn't care one bit if Oscar wanted to be top dog. She was a beagle-basset mix, pretty old, and a little "wide on the sides," as Charles had once said. Ginger never took any notice of other dogs. All she wanted to do was poke along on her short little legs, with her big long ears swaying, sniffing at every single thing she passed. Walking her took practically forever some days.

When Lizzie got home, she took Buddy around to the backyard and made sure the gate to the fence was closed. Then she went inside to find Oscar.

Mom was in the kitchen, scrubbing potatoes in the sink. The Bean stood on a chair beside her with an apron tied around his middle. "I'm helping!" he told Lizzie proudly. His whole front was soaked with water, and he was beaming.

"Where's Oscar?" asked Lizzie.

"In the living room with Charles," said her mom. "Where's Buddy?"

"Out back," Lizzie said. "Can you let him in as soon as Oscar and I leave? I still have one more dog to walk and I'm taking him with me."

Her mother sighed looking down at the potato in her hand. "This is already getting a little tiresome," she said. "All this dog juggling. We really need to find Oscar a home soon. But — did you say you're taking him with you? Are you sure that's a good idea?"

"You want me to find him a home, right? Well, I'm working on it," said Lizzie. "I'm going to introduce him to Ginger. Oscar needs to learn to get along with other dogs, and I think she might be a good place to start."

Mom nodded. "I see. Well, I suppose it's all right, as long as you've cleared it with Ginger's owner," she said.

Lizzie gulped. Mom was right. She'd better ask first. She ran upstairs to find the index cards she kept about each client, and found the one about Ginger. She ran a finger down it, looking for the phone number. Ginger's owner was a pretty young woman with curly hair, named Anjali Davis.

Moments later, Lizzie was on the phone, explaining everything.

"It's fine with me," said Anjali when she'd heard about Oscar. "Nothing fazes Ginger. And she has seemed a little down in the dumps lately. Maybe she could use a friend."

"My aunt told me about some good ways to introduce dogs," Lizzie said before she and Anjali hung up. "Can you take Ginger out into your backyard? I'll be over in five minutes."

She ran back downstairs and found Oscar and Charles playing tug with one of Buddy's toys. "Thanks for taking care of him today," said Lizzie. "I owe you."

"I owe you, Most Perfect Brother," Charles prompted.

Lizzie rolled her eyes. "Right. I owe you, Most Perfect Brother." Then she turned to Oscar and gently took the toy out of his mouth. "C'mon, pal," she told the mustachioed pup. "Let's go. You're going to meet a friend."

She had him sit by the gate to Ginger's backyard. When Anjali came over to say hello, Lizzie made Oscar shake hands with her. Then they opened the gate to let him in and Lizzie took off his leash (Aunt Amanda had told her that some dogs behaved more aggressively when they had leashes on). He let out a tiny woof when he first spotted Ginger, but Lizzie told him to sit again. Ginger plodded calmly forward on her short legs, her ears nearly brushing the ground, and sniffed him for a moment. Oscar went stiff, and Lizzie saw the hair on his back stand up. She got ready to grab his collar in case he started to growl. But instead, he sniffed back. Then his tail began to wag.

Delightful to meet you, madam!

"That worked well," Lizzie said to Anjali as they watched the two dogs touch noses. Now both tails were wagging.

"Ginger usually does best on her own, but she's friendly enough with other dogs," said Anjali. "And she loves people. I like to take her to the yoga studio where I teach. She's very popular there."

Lizzie looked at Oscar. She looked at Ginger. Then she looked at Anjali. "You know . . ." she began. Could it be possible? Could she have found a forever home for Oscar already?

Anjali seemed to read her mind. "Oh, no!" she said, shaking her curly head. "I wouldn't even consider having two dogs. I have my hands full as it is. But you're welcome to bring Oscar along when you walk Ginger, anytime. Maybe he'll pep her up a little bit. All she wants to do lately is sleep."

Lizzie snapped leashes onto both dogs' collars. "Come on, you two," she said. "Let's go for a walk."

It did seem as if Oscar's energy was contagious. Ginger stepped along much more quickly than she usually did. Oscar pranced happily beside her, his bright, intelligent eyes taking in the sights and his nose sniffing busily. Occasionally he and Ginger stopped to play for a moment, but Oscar was always gentle with the older dog.

"You were a good boy, Oscar," said Lizzie as they headed home after the walk. She stopped at the corner to wait for a car to go by and reached into her pocket for a dog biscuit. "Here you go," she said, bending down to give it to the bouncy, bearded pup.

When she straightened up, a flyer on a nearby telephone pole caught her eye — mostly because it featured a picture of a beautiful golden retriever.

Maybe it was about a lost dog. She went over to get a better look at it. "'Premium Pet Dog Walkers,'" she read. "'If you love your pet, hire the best.'" Her heart thudded in her chest. "What is *this*?" she said out loud. She stood and read some more.

Then Lizzie reached up, pulled the flyer down, and stuffed it into her pocket.

CHAPTER SEVEN

"'Keep your beloved pet happy! More than just a daily walk, we offer training, exercise, and stimulation for your dog.'" Back at home, Lizzie hollered into the phone as she read the flyer she'd found to Maria. "Can you believe this?"

On the other end, Maria spoke in soothing tones. "Come on, Lizzie, what's so terrible?" she asked. "So there's another dog-walking business in town."

"And they're advertising in *our* territory, trying to steal *our* customers." Lizzie paced around her mom's office, with Oscar watching from where he lay, curled up under the desk. His eyebrows twitched as he stared at her.

Should I be concerned? There seems to be some trouble.

Lizzie bent down to pet him. She could tell he was upset. So was she.

"Steal our customers?" Maria asked. "Come on, Lizzie."

"Think about it. If they weren't trying to steal our customers, why would they make their price per walk four dollars and fifty cents — fifty cents less than ours — and offer exactly the same thing?" Lizzie smacked her palm on the desk, and Oscar jumped. "Who would *do* this? And how did they know so much about our business, down to the price? We haven't advertised in a long time now."

Maria was silent for a moment. Then she cleared her throat.

"Maria?" Lizzie asked. "Is there something you're not telling me?"

"Well." Maria cleared her throat again. "Remember when you asked me to get some extra help while you were busy training that yappy Pomeranian puppy, Teddy?"

Lizzie rolled her eyes. Why was Maria bringing *that* up again? "Yeah, yeah," she said. "I know. I've been unfair to you. I get it. I'm sorry, and I said so. But what does that —"

"I hired Daphne."

Maria spoke so quickly Lizzie could hardly make out what she said. "What?"

"When I needed extra help, I hired Daphne."

"Daphne *Drake*?" Lizzie yelled. "Are you kidding?" She smacked her palm on the desk again, and Oscar scrambled out from under it. She sat down on the floor and pulled him onto her lap to pet him. Of course Maria wasn't kidding. Of course she was talking about Daphne Drake. What other Daphne did they know? But Daphne? Really? When Maria knew how Lizzie felt about Daphne Drake?

Daphne Drake was the biggest, bossiest know-it-all in fourth grade. For a little while, when they were in a club together, Lizzie had almost started to like Daphne and her friend Brianna. Daphne cared about helping animals, at least. That's what the club had been about, the Caring Club. But the club had fallen apart. Charles said it was because Lizzie had refused to let anybody else be president, but that was ridiculous. Of course she had to be president. For one thing, the club had been her idea. For another, she knew way more about dogs than anyone else in the club — especially Daphne.

Daphne. Lizzie smacked her forehead. This wasn't about the Caring Club. This was about AAA Dynamic Dog Walkers! They had worked hard to build their business, and Lizzie was not about to roll over and play dead. Okay, so Maria had given away all their business secrets to a competitor. So what? They were still the best dog walkers and always would be.

"Lizzie?" Maria asked. "Are you still there?"

"What does Daphne know about training dogs?" Lizzie asked. "How can she even offer that as part of her service?"

"Honestly? I'm not sure *we* should be offering it anymore," Maria said in a small voice. "It's not like we've been doing too much of it lately."

Lizzie gritted her teeth. Why did Maria always have to be *right* about things? Okay, so maybe they hadn't been teaching too many new tricks or working on obedience lessons, like walking nicely on a leash. "We've been pretty busy," was all Lizzie said.

"And Ms. Federico complained the other day that we only took Maxx out for ten minutes. The walks are supposed to be at least twenty minutes long." Maria's voice wasn't so small anymore. "I think we have to shape up, get our act together, or maybe Daphne and Brianna *deserve* to take over our clients."

"Oh, so Brianna's involved, too?" Lizzie asked. "Wait a minute, how did you know that?" She was beginning to feel suspicious. Was Maria in on this whole thing?

"Just a guess," said Maria. "Brianna does everything Daphne does, remember?"

"Arrgh." Lizzie lay down on the rug and let

Oscar lick her face. Maria was right again. About Brianna, and about shaping up. If they weren't careful, they were going to lose all their customers.

Lizzie and Maria talked for a long time, and by the end of their phone call, Lizzie had convinced Maria that they should create a new flyer for AAA Dynamic Dog Walkers and hand it out the next day.

"But you'll have to make it," Maria said before they hung up. "I have homework."

When she put the phone down, Lizzie hugged Oscar and gave him a kiss on the nose. "We've got a job to do tonight, pal," she told him. She had homework, too, but it would have to wait. First she had to save her business. She sat down at the computer and found the file for AAA's first flyer. Then she got busy.

AAA DYNAMIC DOG WALKERS

Always the Best, But Now, Better Than Ever!

Extra-Special Walks. Expert Training.

Excellent Care.

Love Your Dog?

Stick with the Experienced

Dog Walkers.

New low rates: $4.00 per 20-minute walk

CHAPTER EIGHT

Lizzie hummed a happy tune as she dressed for school the next day. She was excited. This felt like a whole new beginning for AAA Dynamic Dog Walkers. And she could hardly wait to start handing out the new flyers.

"Make a negative into a positive," her dad had told her once, when she had complained about being stuck on a bad volleyball team in gym class. She hadn't really understood at the time what he meant, but now she did. Instead of being upset or worried or mad about Daphne's trying to steal their clients, Lizzie had decided to take it as an opportunity to make her and Maria's business better than ever.

She brought the new flyer to school that day, tucked carefully away in the back of her notebook. At recess time, she pulled Maria aside and they waited until everybody else had left the room. Lizzie even checked the cubby area in the back of their classroom, to make sure nobody — like Daphne Drake, for example — was listening. She felt like a spy with top-secret documents in her possession. "What do you think?" she whispered. She opened her notebook to show Maria the flyer.

Maria nodded. "Nice. But that's a pretty big drop in our price, isn't it?"

Lizzie waved a hand. "If we add a few more clients, it won't matter if our price is lower. In the long run, we'll make even more money. Ms. Dobbins will be so happy." Ms. Dobbins was the director of Caring Paws, the animal shelter where

Lizzie volunteered sometimes. She and Maria had pledged to donate 10 percent of their earnings to the shelter.

"More clients?" Maria stared at her. "We're barely keeping up with the ones we already have."

"Do you want to save our business or not?" Lizzie demanded.

For a moment, Maria didn't answer. She looked down at her sneakers. "I guess so," she finally mumbled.

After school that day, Lizzie met Maria at their usual corner. Maria had already picked up Tank and Atlas. "You're late," she said.

"Sorry," said Lizzie. "I stopped to stick up a few flyers." She held up a sheaf of papers. She had pinned a few to telephone poles and stuffed some more into mailboxes at the ends of people's driveways. "But I'm here now." She took Tank's leash.

"And I didn't bring any puppies with me, notice?" She grinned at Maria.

Lizzie had set the timer feature on her watch, to make sure they gave each dog at least a twenty-minute walk. She had stuffed her favorite dog-training book into her backpack, along with the flyers, tape, and pushpins. She had looked through the book the night before and stuck Post-it notes on all the pages that had good training exercises or tips, and during their walks that day she and Maria tried out at least one with every dog. Lizzie also made sure to give each dog some special attention: an ear rub for Tank, a belly scratching for Scruffy, and hugs and extra pats for Pixie and Pogo, the twin poodles.

They handed out flyers to their customers, or stuck them in their mailboxes. "Huh," said Ms. Federico when she read the one they gave her.

"You're lowering your price. That's terrific! How often does *that* happen?"

Maria shot Lizzie a look, but Lizzie just ignored it and smiled at Ms. Federico. "Just trying to do our best to give you great service," she said.

At the end of the afternoon, Lizzie volunteered to walk Ginger on her own. "I'll take Oscar over again," she told Maria. "I think it was really good for him to be around another dog, and Ginger seemed to enjoy the company."

She went home and picked up Oscar, then headed off to Ginger's house, posting flyers along the way. She put one up on a telephone pole, handed one to a teenage boy who was walking a beagle, then stuffed a couple into mailboxes. She was two doors away from Ginger's house, putting a flyer into another mailbox, when she spotted a mailman across the street. She smiled and waved, wondering if he carried dog biscuits in his bag, the way Rita, their mail deliverer, did. Rita was so friendly, and she loved dogs. She would always stop to ask about whatever new foster puppy Lizzie was walking, and give it pets and treats. Rita hadn't met Oscar yet, but Lizzie knew she would love him when she did.

But instead of smiling and waving back, the mailman trotted across the street toward Lizzie, frowning. "You're not allowed to do that, you know," he said, waving a hand at the flyer she was stuffing into a red mailbox. "Only employees of the United States Postal Service can put mail into mailboxes."

"It's just a flyer," Lizzie said, holding it out to show him, "for my dog-walking business."

He didn't even glance at it. "You're breaking the law," he said. "Regulation 3.1.3 states clearly that anyone putting anything other than US mail into a mailbox can be prosecuted and fined."

"Oh." Lizzie let her arm drop. This mailman wasn't *anything* like Rita. In fact, the way he'd charged over and growled at her reminded her of the way Oscar had behaved when he spotted Bowser that day at Aunt Amanda's. "Sorry. I won't do it anymore," she said, looking down at the ground.

"I imagine you won't, now that you know it's against the law," said the mailman, and now his voice was a little gentler. He reached into his mailbag. "Would your pup like a biscuit?"

Lizzie looked down at Oscar. He thumped his tail on the sidewalk.

I believe I heard the word "biscuit" mentioned. Does that mean —

"Sure," said Lizzie. She didn't bother explaining that Oscar wasn't exactly her pup. The mailman bent down and gave Oscar a bone-shaped dog biscuit.

"Good boy," he murmured. "Aren't you a good-looking gentleman?"

Lizzie smiled to herself. Everybody loved dogs. Maybe this mailman wasn't such a meanie after all. Maybe he only *acted* grouchy sometimes, just like Oscar. "His name is Oscar," she said.

"Well, Oscar," said the mailman. "How about one more biscuit?"

Oscar's tail thumped again. He put up a paw.

"Oh, you shake hands, too? What a smartie." The mailman dug out another biscuit and handed it over.

Lizzie was still smiling as she walked up to Ginger's house. She told Oscar to sit and knocked on the door.

Anjali was *not* smiling when she opened the door. In fact, she looked as if she'd been crying. "Oh, Lizzie," she said. "I almost forgot you were coming. I'm so glad you're here. Ginger is not doing well today. She's not doing well at all."

CHAPTER NINE

"Not doing well? What happened?" Lizzie asked. "Is she sick? Is it catching? Maybe I shouldn't bring Oscar in."

Anjali shook her head and opened the door wider. "No, it's okay. Please come in. I think Ginger would like to see Oscar." She waved Lizzie into the living room. Ginger was curled up on the rug, next to a low couch that was covered in a brightly colored cloth. When Lizzie and Oscar went into the room, Ginger struggled to her feet and, panting, came over to touch noses with Oscar. Lizzie watched closely in case Oscar growled, but all he did was sniff Ginger and wag his tail. Ginger wagged her tail, too.

"Sit down, please," Anjali said to Lizzie. She pulled a tissue from a box and blew her nose. "Aww, that's so sweet," she said, pointing to Oscar.

Oscar was licking the side of Ginger's face, kissing her sweetly and gently.

"It's as if he knows," said Anjali. She sniffled and blew her nose again.

"Knows what?" Lizzie thought Ginger looked okay. Sure, maybe she was moving even more slowly than usual, but other than that she seemed fine.

Anjali sighed. "Last night, Ginger didn't want any dinner. And this morning, I could barely even get her to drink some water. She doesn't want to go outside, but she can't seem to settle down inside, either. She just paces around the house, panting. Then she flops down for a few moments. Then she gets up again. I called the vet, and we went to see her this afternoon."

"Well, that's good," said Lizzie. "You go to Dr. Gibson, right? I'm sure she can help."

Anjali shook her head. "Not this time," she said. "Ginger is fifteen years old, you know. She's had a good life, but she has been slowing down for a long time. Dr. Gibson thinks she's —" Anjali broke down again, burying her face in her hands.

"Ohhh," said Lizzie. Suddenly, she understood. She put her hand on Anjali's back. "You mean —"

Anjali nodded as she blew her nose one more time. "What Ginger has isn't catching. It's just old age, and she's probably in her last days now. Dr. Gibson said all we can do is make sure she is comfortable and not in pain."

Lizzie nodded. "How can I help?" she asked.

"You probably don't need me to walk her anymore, since she doesn't even want to go out."

"No, you're right," said Anjali. "I can take care of that. But I would love it if you could be here when I'm out teaching my classes. I don't think I should bring her with me to the yoga studio anymore, but I don't want to leave her alone any more than I have to. And look." She pointed at the dogs. "I think Oscar really helps her relax and calm down."

Sure enough, Ginger lay quietly on the rug now, snoring gently, while Oscar lay next to her, occasionally putting out a paw as if to comfort the older dog.

"Just tell me your schedule," said Lizzie. "I'll do whatever I can."

"Thanks," said Anjali. She reached over and picked up a scrapbook from the coffee table. "Want to see what Ginger looked like when she was a puppy? I was just about your age when my dad brought her home one summer day. Look!"

Lizzie leaned over to see the picture Anjali was pointing to. "Oh, cute!" she said. A little girl with blond braids and a wide grin stood under a tree, holding a tiny brown-and-black puppy whose ears looked three times too big.

Anjali smiled down at the picture. "I didn't have any brothers or sisters, so Ginger became my best friend in the world." She touched the picture. "I told her all my secrets, and she went everywhere I went. Well, maybe not to school. Except one day when she followed me there and Mrs. Dempsey let her stay in our classroom until my mom came to pick her up. . . ."

Lizzie heard a lot of stories about Ginger that week. Every day, after school and in the evenings, Lizzie and Oscar spent as much time as they could at Anjali's house. Maria understood. She told Lizzie not to worry, that she'd make sure their clients' dogs got walked. Lizzie's family understood, too — even though Charles did make Lizzie call him a different name each day, in exchange for taking over some of her chores.

Some days at Anjali's it was just Lizzie and Oscar sitting quietly with Ginger. Sometimes Anjali was there and they sat on the couch together, looking at pictures. Anjali told Lizzie about how Ginger had helped her survive middle school. She showed her pictures from her senior prom night in high school: a boy and a girl all dressed up in formal clothes, with Ginger sitting between them on a porch swing. And she told Lizzie how hard it had been to leave Ginger when she went off to college, and how wonderful it was to see her again whenever she went home for vacations. "And now we live together again, and it's been so great having my best friend with me," Anjali said, looking fondly at Ginger.

Ginger and Oscar seemed like best friends, too. From the moment he entered the house, Oscar paid attention to nobody and nothing but Ginger. He was by her side every second, lying curled up next to her and gazing at her with his wise eyes. Lizzie couldn't believe how patient and gentle he was with the older dog. She knew now that she would be able to find Oscar a wonderful forever home — somewhere. He had proved that he could get along with at least one dog, so maybe he didn't have to be the only dog in a family after all.

Each day, Ginger seemed to fade a little bit. She wasn't eating or drinking at all anymore, and by Thursday she barely even lifted her head when Lizzie and Oscar arrived.

On Friday, when Lizzie got home from school, her mom met her at the door. Before she even said a word, Lizzie knew. Just by looking at her mother's sad face, she knew that Anjali had called to say that Ginger had died. Mom pulled Lizzie into her arms. "I'm sorry, honey. I know how hard this is."

Lizzie sobbed into her mother's chest. She wasn't even sure who she was crying for. Ginger? Anjali? The little girl in that picture, so happy with her puppy? And what about Oscar? He was going to miss his friend. It wasn't fair. It just wasn't fair at all. Why, oh why, couldn't dogs live as long as people did?

CHAPTER TEN

"What are *they* doing here?" Lizzie whispered to Maria.

"Shhh! It's starting." Maria pointed to Anjali, who stood quietly beneath the blossom-covered boughs of an old apple tree. The pink and white flowers gave off a sweet smell as Lizzie came to stand closer. Oscar sniffed at the air as if he enjoyed their sweetness, too.

Anjali smiled at the small group of people gathered nearby, and spoke in a soft voice. "Thanks to all of you for coming. I know you cared for Ginger and I wanted us to say good-bye to her together." She gestured at a mound of dirt under the apple tree. It was sprinkled with apple blossoms, and a bouquet of daffodils in a blue jar sat near a wooden plaque. "My dad helped me bury Ginger, and he made that beautiful plaque for her, too."

Lizzie felt the tears start to come when she saw the carved letters. "F NNC⬚NF ⬚ HMF DQ," they read. Ginger's collar hung on one corner of the sign. Lizzie tucked Oscar's leash under her elbow and rummaged in her pocket. Where were those tissues? Her mom had passed her a handful as she had left the house that morning for Ginger's memorial.

Next to her, Brianna leaned over and whispered, sniffling, "Can I have one of those?"

Lizzie gave her a tissue. She still didn't know what Brianna and Daphne were doing there, but now was not the time to ask. Anjali was talking again.

"I wrote a long letter to Ginger, sort of a love letter, I guess," she said. "I buried it with her. But I wanted all of you to have a chance to tell Ginger what you loved about her, too." She held out her hands to the people on either side of her, a woman Lizzie recognized as a neighbor, and — hey! — wasn't that the grouchy mailman?

"Let's all hold hands and have a moment of silent reflection," Anjali was saying. "And then if anyone wants to speak, they are welcome to."

Lizzie turned to look at Maria. They clasped hands and gave each other sad smiles. Maria squeezed Lizzie's hand. "He's being so good," she whispered with a glance down at Oscar.

Sure enough, Oscar was sitting quietly by Lizzie's feet. She had made sure to take him for a long walk that morning, to tire him out. He glanced up at Lizzie from beneath his bushy brows.

This is such a serious occasion. And where's my lovely long-eared lady friend?

Lizzie turned to Brianna and held out her other hand. Brianna smiled and took it. Then they all closed their eyes and the yard was quiet, except for a breeze rustling the apple blossoms and the chirping of a bird.

Lizzie thought of Ginger's sweet face, and of how soft her long ears were, and of the way she and Oscar would lie next to each other.

"Good-bye, dear Ginger," Anjali said, breaking the silence.

Lizzie had to blow her nose again and wipe her eyes.

"Would anyone like to speak?" Anjali asked.

Lizzie was surprised when Daphne stepped forward. "Brianna and I met Ginger when we started to go to Anjali's Yoga for Youngsters class.

She was so sweet the way she lay next to Anjali's mat, waiting patiently for class to end. Brianna and I would always spend some time with her afterward. I loved to pet her silky ears."

Next to Lizzie, Brianna sniffled. Lizzie handed her another tissue. So that was why they were there. Lizzie thought about what Daphne had said. Ginger really was a very patient dog — but it had not always been easy to be patient with her. Lizzie had never tugged on Ginger's leash or yelled at her, but sometimes she had been tempted to, when Ginger was taking forever to go around the block.

"Ginger was forgiving." Someone else was speaking now. The mailman! "If I ran out of biscuits by the time I got to her house, she never held it against me," he went on. "She was always happy to see me, biscuit or no biscuit."

Lizzie looked at Maria. Her friend sure was forgiving. No matter how mad Maria was at Lizzie, she always got over it. Lizzie squeezed Maria's hand again. She vowed to try to be more forgiving herself. Then she turned back to the circle. She felt like she wanted to say something. "Ginger was kind," she said. "I never saw her be mean to another dog or a person. She welcomed Oscar into her house, even though he isn't always the easiest dog to get along with."

Anjali nodded and smiled at Lizzie. "Oscar was there for Ginger in her last days. I will never forget that."

A few other people spoke, and then Anjali went around the circle, giving each of them a daffodil. As she passed out the flowers, she took a moment to hold each person's hands and say a few private words. When she came to Lizzie, she said, "Thank you, Lizzie, for all the time you took to make Ginger's last days happier." She knelt down to pet Oscar. "And thank you, Oscar. You are a very special dog."

Lizzie had to stop herself from asking if Anjali would like to adopt Oscar. She knew it was much too soon for that. She looked over at the grouchy mailman, thinking that she ought to talk to him about Oscar. They had gotten along well — maybe because they were a little alike. Was he interested in owning a dog?

Maria touched Lizzie's elbow. "I have to tell you something," she whispered. "You know I needed help when you were spending all that time with Ginger, right?"

"Sure." Lizzie saw Maria cut her eyes toward Brianna and Daphne, who were standing together near Ginger's grave. "Oh," she said. "You hired them?"

Maria nodded. "And they were great, too. They both really love dogs. They were responsible and patient and good to work with."

Lizzie closed her eyes for a moment. She took a deep breath. She thought about patience, and forgiveness, and kindness, and the example Ginger had set. Then she opened her eyes and looked at her friend. "So why are we trying to fight them?" she asked. "Why don't we just ask if they'd like to join our business? We sure could use the help."

Maria grinned. "I was hoping you'd say that," she said. She threw her arms around Lizzie. "It's really the perfect solution. Let's go ask them."

Later, as Lizzie and Maria and Daphne and Brianna sat beneath the apple tree talking about plans for their business, Anjali came over and tapped Lizzie on the shoulder. "Can we talk for a minute?" she asked.

Lizzie and Anjali went to sit on the back steps of the house. Oscar lay down by their feet. "I have a favor to ask you," said Anjali, reaching out to scratch Oscar between the ears.

"Me?" said Lizzie. "Sure. Anything."

"I was wondering if I could keep Oscar for a while," Anjali said. "I — I just miss Ginger so much. And somehow, after all that time they spent together, I feel like Oscar has some of her spirit. I think he would be a comfort to me — just the way he was to her." Oscar seemed to sense what she was saying. He stood up and put his head on Anjali's lap.

"Of course," said Lizzie. "I was actually wondering if you might be interested in adopting him, but I thought it was too soon."

"Well, I can't promise for sure right now," said Anjali, smiling down at Oscar, "but my guess is that if he comes for a few days, he'll end up stay-ing forever. I understand that he needs some help learning to get along with other dogs, but I'd be willing to put in the time to work on that. It would be a good distraction for me."

Lizzie reached into her pocket for another tis-sue. She was crying again, but this time her tears were happy ones.

"Are you okay?" Suddenly, Maria was at Lizzie's side.

Lizzie nodded and blew her nose into a tissue. "I'm fine," she said. She told her friend that Oscar was going to stay with Anjali for a while.

Lizzie and Maria turned to look at Anjali, who was kneeling to hug the wiry little pup. Oscar licked Anjali's face and wagged his stumpy tail.

"I think Oscar may have found the perfect

home," said Lizzie and Maria at exactly the same time.

"Pickle Jinx!" yelled Maria.

Lizzie smiled. She didn't have to think hard to come up with the name she'd like Maria to call her. "Best Friend Forever," she said.

PUPPY TIPS

Aggressive dogs can be a real problem. Oscar is not exactly aggressive, but he does not get along with some dogs. Other dogs can be aggressive toward people. Some dogs, like guard dogs, are trained to be aggressive. Others are just naturally that way or had bad experiences when they were young.

Many dogs can be trained *out* of being aggressive — though it's not always easy. It's good to catch this problem early, as in Oscar's case, and get help from a professional trainer, a vet, or a dog behaviorist. If you notice that your puppy or dog growls or snaps at people or other dogs (not in a playful way), do not encourage the behavior, and talk to your parents about getting help.

Dear Reader,

Many of you have written to tell me how sorry you were to hear of my dog Django's death from old age. And many of you have told me about losing beloved dogs, cats, or other pets of your own. That's why I wanted to write about a dog who died, even though it is not the easiest or happiest subject. As pet owners, this is one of the hardest things we have to deal with: saying good-bye.

I believe it is important to treasure our pets while they are alive and make sure they are happy and safe. If we know we have given them good lives, it is easier to let them go when the time comes. And every pet you've had will stay alive in your heart for the rest of your life. I will never forget Tracker, Jenny, Willy, Ace, Jack, Molly, Junior, and Django, my beloved cats and dogs.

Yours from the Puppy Place,
Ellen Miles

THE PUPPY PLACE

DON'T MISS THE NEXT PUPPY PLACE ADVENTURE!

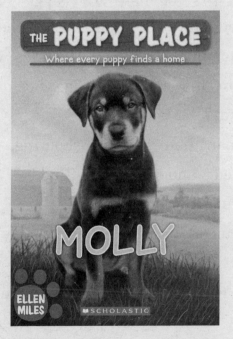

Here's a peek at MOLLY!

Mom always said Charles was good with little kids. Charles was proud of that. He was good with puppies, too. Not just his own puppy, Buddy, but lots of other puppies, too. The Petersons — Charles and his older sister, Lizzie, and the Bean and Mom and Dad — were a foster family for puppies. They took care of puppies who needed homes, and helped find forever families for each one.

Now, hugging the Bean, Charles whispered again into his ear, "Let's go home and see Buddy, okay?"

The Bean had stopped shouting, and now he nodded and smiled. "Buddy," he said. "Buddy-Puddy-Muddy-Wuddy."

"That's right," said Charles. "Buddy's waiting for us."

Miss Penny smiled. "You're a terrific big brother, Charles. I bet you're a huge help to your parents."

Charles shrugged. Behind him, his mom put her hands on his shoulders. "He sure is," she said. "He'll be a help on our field trip next week, too. I've asked him to come along when we go to Fable Farm." Mom had signed up to be a field trip helper. So far she'd gone along on the day care's trips to the library, the firehouse, and a bakery. But this time she was in charge. She was planning a special trip for the Penny's Place kids, a visit to a local farm where they had ducks and geese and sheep and all kinds of vegetables and flowers, too. Charles was going to get to leave school early that day just so he could come along.

"Oh, that's terrific," said Miss Penny. "We're going to have a big group that day."

"Charles and the Bean and I will go to the farm in the next few days," Mom told Miss Penny. "We thought it might be a good idea to check things out there ahead of time so we can plan our visit."

"Wonderful," said Miss Penny.

Just then, the Bean pulled himself away from Charles's hug and pointed high up in the air. "Up, up, up, up, up," he yelled.

Everyone turned to look. Daniel waved and grinned at them — from on top of the fridge.

"How does he *do* that?" Mom asked. "I never even saw —"

Miss Penny just laughed as she strode over to lift Daniel down. "You can't take your eyes off him for a second," she said to Mom and Charles. To Daniel and the Bean, she said, "Go get your things from your cubbies and help Annabelle straighten up the block corner. It's almost time to go home."

"How do *you* do it?" Mom asked Miss Penny, once Daniel and the Bean had been shooed into the other room. "I mean, there's something happening every minute here, but you always keep your cool. And the kids seem to respond when you tell them to do something. I think the Bean listens to you better than he listens to me."

Miss Penny shrugged. "I'm used to it, I guess," she said. "But there's one thing I'm not used to, and I think I need your help." She gestured toward a door at the back of the kitchen. "She's out here."

"She? Who?" asked Charles, as he followed along, curious.

Miss Penny unlocked the door with a key she pulled out of her pocket. "Her name is Molly," she said, as she pushed open the door to a small pantry.

Charles only had one moment to wonder why Miss Penny would be keeping a little girl in that room. As the door swung open, he realized that Molly was not a little girl.

Molly was a puppy.

ABOUT THE AUTHOR

Ellen Miles loves dogs, which is why she has a great time writing the Puppy Place books. And guess what? She loves cats, too! (In fact, her very first pet was a beautiful tortoiseshell cat named Jenny.) That's why she came up with the Kitty Corner series. Ellen lives in Vermont and loves to be outdoors every day, walking, biking, skiing, or swimming, depending on the season. She also loves to read, cook, explore her beautiful state, play with dogs, and hang out with friends and family.

Visit Ellen at www.ellenmiles.net.